AWARD PUBLICATIONS – LONDON

Debbie's visit to the countryside

GILBERT DELAHAYE - MARCEL MARLIER

One summer Aunt Lucy wrote to Debbie's parents. "Would Debbie like to spend a few days with me here in the country-side? There'll be lots for her to do."

Mummy and Daddy said yes. So full of excitement, Debbie packed her suitcase and set off with Rusty, her little dog.

As soon as they arrived Jasper, Aunt Lucy's dalmatian, came rushing out to welcome them.

"How long are you staying, Rusty?" he asked.

"At least a week."

"Hooray! I can teach you to chase rabbits and to roll in the grass. We're going to be real friends, just you wait and see."

Besides Jasper Aunt Lucy had a bright green parrot called Amigo.

"What a lovely day, what a lovely day! Let's go for a ride in the car!" he squawked. He said anything that came into his head. And sometimes he winked. Debbie thought he was very funny.

There was a birdhouse in the garden. It needed fresh paint so Aunt Lucy gave Debbie the paint and a long brush. She had to be very careful because the birds kept flying at her from all directions.

Some of the doves were not at all afraid of Debbie.

"Come and see this little girl perched on a ladder!" one called to the others from her shoulder.

"Take care your feathers don't get stuck in the paint!" warned Debbie.

The cat from the farm was doing somersaults on the ladder.

"Go away!" cried the doves. "This isn't your garden."

Just then a duck came wandering into the garden.

"I'm going to catch you," called Debbie.

"Not on your life... quack, quack,..."

"Careful you don't trample on Aunt Lucy's flowers! Come back here!" cried Debbie.

But the duck wriggled away.

A boy came running in to help her.

"It's Pip, my duck. He must have flown over the hedge," he said.

"My name's Christopher. I live next door on the farm. I'll catch him for you in no time."

It's quite difficult to hold a duck in your arms, but Christopher just managed it. Pip flapped his wings at him.

"Let me go!" he quacked.

Then it began to rain.

"Would you like to go looking for frogs?" Christopher asked.

"Frogs? Where?"

"In the pool. I've seen some there."

They took Pip home, then they went to the pool. "What a lovely splashy place," said Debbie.

Next day Debbie's mother called to find out how she was.

"I'm fine, and so's Aunt Lucy," Debbie told her. "How are you? Christopher who lives next door has got a duck called Pip. I like them both... Yesterday I repainted the birdhouse, and then we went looking for frogs.

Today it's raining so we can't go out but Aunt Lucy found lots of her old hats and coats for dressing up.

Rusty has been playing with Jasper... I found an old record player in the attic and it still works..."

By now the rain was streaming down outside. "It's really raining cats and dogs today," laughed Debbie to Rusty and Jasper. The dogs were very bored indoors and jumped up at Debbie, whining for her to play with them.

"I know," she said, "Let's blow bubbles. I'll go and make some."

Rusty and Jasper ran around, barking happily when they saw the first bubbles floating from the bowl of soapy water.

Debbie watched the stream of bubbles in delight, as they shimmered and floated away lighter than feathers. Then... poof... one by one they burst.

The dogs looked so funny as they tried to catch them.

Next morning at breakfast Amigo greeted them as usual; "What a lovely day, what a lovely day! Let's go for a ride in the car!"

"Amigo's right for once," laughed Aunt Lucy. "I've just seen a rainbow in the sky and that's a good sign. Let's drive to the mountains for the day. By the time we get there the sun will have dried up all the rain."

On the way the car suddenly spluttered to a halt. "I think we've run out of petrol," said Aunt Lucy. But no, it was all right, a man helped them push, the engine gave a cough, and off they went again.

Debbie was amazed to find so many different wild flowers
growing on the mountain slopes. "What a chance this is to start
a pressed flower collection," she thought, and she began to pick
a few of each kind, taking care not to crush the lacy leaves and
delicate flowers.

Jasper laughed as he watched her trying to catch the blue butterflies in her net. She did not want to hurt them, and let them go as soon as she had studied their brilliant colours. She thought they were the most beautiful things she had ever seen.

It was nearly time to go home.

"Look down there," called Christopher. "One of the goats has wandered off from the rest of the herd. She might hurt herself."

"We'd better go and tell the farmer," said Debbie.

Then Christopher suddenly stumbled and gave a cry.

"What's happened? Have you hurt yourself?"

"My trousers are caught in the barbed wire. I'm stuck," he said.

Very very carefully Debbie unhooked the wire.

Safely back at home, Aunt Lucy mended some torn clothes while Debbie cleaned the grazes on Christopher's knee.

"Do you think the goat was really lost?" asked Debbie anxiously.

"I expect she knew her own way home," said Aunt Lucy.

They all agreed they had had a marvellous day.

Christopher asked Debbie what she was going to do with all the flowers she had picked.

"I'm going to start a pressed flower collection."

He watched fascinated as she placed the flowers between pieces of thick paper and put them in a special press.

She was careful not to damage the petals and leaves.

"Later, when they are dry, I shall stick them onto sheets of plain paper," Debbie said. "Then I shall write the name beside each flower and the spot where I found it. I'll bind the sheets together with ribbon to make a book. It will be a lovely reminder of my visit to the countryside."

It was time for Debbie to leave. She felt a little sad as she kissed Christopher goodbye, but she was looking forward to telling her mother and father all about the different animals and birds and flowers she had seen. They would find it hard to believe that the countryside could be such an exciting place. Besides, she knew it would not be so very long before she saw Christopher and Aunt Lucy again!